Thomas Nicholson

An Essay on Yellow Fever

AF285326

SALZWASSER
VERLAG

Thomas Nicholson

An Essay on Yellow Fever

1st Edition | ISBN: 978-3-75257-760-0

Place of Publication: Frankfurt am Main, Germany

Year of Publication: 2022

Salzwasser Verlag GmbH, Germany.

Reprint of the original, first published in 1866.

AN ESSAY

ON

YELLOW FEVER.

AN ESSAY

ON

YELLOW FEVER.

COMPRISING

THE HISTORY OF THAT DISEASE,

AS IT APPEARED IN THE ISLAND OF ANTIGUA IN
THE YEARS 1835, 1839, AND 1842,

WITH

AN APPENDIX CONTINUING THE HISTORY TO 1853.

SECOND EDITION.

LONDON:

M DCCC LXVI.

PREFACE.

THE first edition of the following Essay consisted only of a few copies, which were printed for private distribution. These have been long out of print, and the Author, in compliance with the advice of friends, has been induced to reprint the Essay. Some of the opinions which were at first modestly suggested, out of deference to authority, have been established by subsequent experience. Blood-letting, as an abortive treatment in the early stage of the ardent type of the disease, is not in such favour as it was in the early part of the present century.

The solution of such disputed questions can only be settled by a faithful record of cases.

Dr. Parkes has wisely said, "the most valuable addition any one could at present make, to our knowledge of tropical fevers, would be a simple record of all the cases in an epidemic. These cases should be observed with the keen tact of a Chomel, and recorded with the fidelity of a Louis. We want no explanation or word of comment added to them; we want merely the cases."—*Brit. and For. Med.-Chir. Review*, October, 1850.

It was in the spirit of these remarks, that the Author was first induced to draw up a history of the epidemics which had come under his own notice, and although he is conscious now that his powers of observation were not then trained for the task, and that there are many omissions which he would gladly have an opportunity of supplying, yet he hopes the observations recorded may not be without value.

During his absence from Antigua, in 1859, another outbreak of yellow fever occurred, and, on this occasion his son, Dr. A. Nicholson, had an opportunity of verifying the fact of the presence of albumen in the urine in most cases.

14, BLANDFORD SQUARE, N.W.

AN ESSAY.

THE subject of the following Essay is that peculiar form of fever which, under the different names of Yellow Fever, Vomito Negro, Vomito Prieto, and Bulam Fever, has been known to the English and Spanish colonists on both sides of the Atlantic for nearly a century; occurring at distant and uncertain intervals, and producing great mortality, especially amongst Europeans who have resided but a short time in these parts. It has been described by nosologists under the terms of Typhus Icterodes, *Cullen;* Synochus Icterodes, *Young;* Epanetus Malignus Flavus, *Good;* and more recently by Dr. Copland, from its pathological characters, Hæmagastric Pestilence. The term *Hæmalytic Epidemic* of the Atlantic shores would, in my opinion, express more accurately the peculiar features of the disease; but I am unwilling to make any addi-

B

tions to its nomenclature, which, after all, is of little importance.

I had been thirteen years in Antigua before I had an opportunity of witnessing a single case of this disease, although severe and fatal cases of bilious remittent were met with in malarious localities every year, and in some seasons prevailed as an epidemic over the whole island— as, for instance, in the year 1823, a short account of which, by my friend Dr. Musgrave, will be found in the twenty-eighth volume of the "Edinburgh Medical and Surgical Journal" for 1827. Yet, although the mortality from this epidemic was very great, in no instance did black vomit occur; and, from the information I could collect on the subject, I have every reason to believe that *vomito prieto* was not known amongst civilians in that colony from 1816 till 1835. I exclude, of course, the cases of the *Pyramus*, and two other men-of-war, which arrived at English Harbour with yellow fever in 1821 and 1822.

Being taught in my early years, by the writings of Bancroft, Fergusson, and others, and by the oral instructions of the medical gentlemen under whom I served in the West Indies, to regard yellow fever as a more severe grade only of the endemic fever, I was often puzzled to account for the absence of this peculiar symptom in all the cases I had seen; and I was sometimes inclined to hazard an opinion that, after all, Chisholm might be right. Subsequent experience has convinced me that yellow fever differs as much from bilious remittent as the epidemic or Asiatic cholera differs from sporadic or English cholera; but I never met with any circumstance that could prove its propagation by contagion.* The following history will show that it broke out in St. John's in 1835, at a time when our harbour was almost destitute of shipping, and when, consequently, we had no intercourse with the neighbouring islands; and, although convalescents were frequently carried into the country for change of air, the disease was not propagated in the rural districts.

* Since the above was written, indisputable proofs have accumulated of the infectious nature of yellow fever when it occurs on board ship, in badly-ventilated barracks and hospitals, or in crowded dwellings in seaport towns.

On the 12th August, 1835, the island of
Antigua was visited by a severe hurricane,
which did great damage to the buildings in
town and country, but more so to the vessels in
the harbour of St. John's, most of which were
driven on shore and destroyed, or so much dis-
abled as to be unfit for sea. A person inex-
perienced in these tropical tornadoes can scarcely
form an adequate idea of the fury with which
the wind raged for a few hours. The barometer
fell in the course of one hour and twenty minutes
1·5 inch, a rapidity of descent which, as far as I
can learn, has not been equalled in any former
hurricane on record. The centre of this whirl-
wind moved at a steady rate in a westerly direction, being felt some hours later at each island
in that course; and, strange to say, it was
scarcely felt at all forty miles to the south of
Antigua. Before the occurrence of the hurricane the inhabitants were tolerably healthy—at
least they were free from any acute or febrile
diseases; but the weather was dry and sultry,
and dyspeptic complaints were more than
usually prevalent. The excitement, however,
occasioned by the hurricane, and the vigorous

exertions required to repair its effects, dispelled these anomalous complaints, and for some weeks subsequent to the gale the number on the sick list was small. The state of the weather was not similarly ameliorated by the atmospheric commotion. The heat was greater, the wind variable and more westerly than usual, and there were frequent showers of rain. The sea, which rose in the gale above its usual level, aided by the wind, had deposited a great quantity of marine organic matters and vegetable rubbish about the wharves and precincts of the town bounded by the harbour; and it was remarked by the inhabitants in that quarter that the smell arising from the sea, particularly at night, was peculiarly offensive.

On the 20th September I was called to a case of fever in a young Irishman, who resided in a house on one of the wharves, which had suffered greatly in the gale, and was then undergoing repair. It proved rather an obstinate case, the headache, gastric irritability, and rachialgia, being very severe; but it terminated favourably. When, each successive day, one or two other cases were added to my list, I began to suspect that we were about to have a visitation of some epidemic, and it is recorded in my note-book at that time as *epidemic gastric fever*. It is worthy of remark, that it broke out in the same locality, and much in the same way, as the "Dandy Fever," that peculiar arthritic exanthem, which I have described in vol. xxxi. of the "Edinburgh Medical and Surgical Journal" for 1829, p. 115.

I was attacked myself on the 7th October, and during my confinement, which was only three days, the more malignant characters of the disease were developed; but it was not till the 10th October that we had a case of black vomit, when the true nature of the epidemic was discovered. It may be necessary to mention, however, that none of the medical gentlemen engaged in practice in St. John's at that time had ever seen a case of yellow fever, otherwise the discovery might have been made earlier.

The epidemic continued to increase till the first week of November, after which it gradually declined, and by the end of December had nearly disappeared. The last death occurred on the 24th of that month, in the wife of a Moravian missionary, who arrived in the island from England on the 9th, and was attacked on the 15th. During that period I had attended two hundred and twenty cases, of whom seventy-five were Europeans, sixty-five white Creoles, and eighty coloured persons. Of the Europeans, twelve died, of whom ten had not been in the island twelve months. None of the Creoles or native whites died; but two of the mixed race sunk under peculiar circumstances.

In June, 1839, yellow fever again made its appearance, attacking only those young men who had come to the island during the interval. This epidemic was of a more open or inflammatory type than the former, and copious venesection was practised with much success.

In September, 1842, another invasion of the disease took place, and continued till the middle of November, during which time I attended forty-three cases—viz., twenty-two Europeans, twenty white Creoles, and one of the mixed race. The Europeans had only been a few years in the colony, and of these eight died; the Creoles were chiefly children, of whom three died.

On all these occasions it is remarkable that

the epidemic was confined to the town of St.
John's; and although our practice extends over
twenty-eight estates, on each of which several
white persons resided, who were unprotected by
a former attack, none of these took the disease.

SYMPTOMS.

In private practice the physician has few
opportunities of witnessing the premonitory
symptoms of fever, except in his own person;
and therefore I will only describe what I myself
experienced. I got up in the morning with an
unusual feeling of lassitude, and with some un-
easiness in the head, and pain in the back and
limbs. I had no sense of chilliness, nor was
the temperature of the surface increased; but I
had much thirst, and the swallowing of liquids
was immediately followed by nausea and copious
perspiration. The pulse was weak and variable,
and much accelerated by the slightest exertion.
Notwithstanding these symptoms, I continued
to discharge my professional duties till 10 P.M.,
when the pains in the head and back became
almost intolerable, the vomiting incessant, and

the febrile excitement fully developed. The paroxysm continued for thirty-six hours, when it left me in a state of extreme exhaustion, with a furred tongue, which lasted for several days, and a yellow hue in the skin and conjunctiva.

Such was the mild form in which the epidemic manifested itself in natives and persons who had been long resident in the West Indies; but in others it assumed a highly malignant character, producing a rapid dissolution of the blood, which exuded into the mucous canals, and sometimes even through the pores of the skin; and it frequently terminated in death by asthenia or coma, on the third, fifth, or seventh day.

Three varieties of this malignant type were observable. The first I shall term the *ardent;* the second, the *adynamic;* the third, the *congestive* or *apyretic.*

I. The ARDENT form was ushered in with the usual symptoms of a febrile attack — slight rigors, or only a coldness of the extremities, headache with suffusion of the eyes, general lassitude, and pain in the back. In a few hours,

these symptoms were followed by a hot burning
skin, great throbbing of the carotid and temporal arteries, intense headache and rachialgia;
pulse from 90 to 120, full and strong; incessant
thirst, and vomiting of fluid, which often exceeded in quantity what was swallowed. The
bowels were obstinately constipated, the urine
high-coloured, and sometimes entirely suppressed. The discharges from the bowels, produced by medicine, generally resembled ditch-
water, being free from all appearance of bile. The
blood drawn at the first visit presented no unusual character. About the second day, the patient
complained much of flatulency in the stomach,
occasioning frequent efforts to expel it, which
Dr. Dewees, of Philadelphia, has very graphically
described as a *vomiting of wind.* There was
also a sense of stricture about the cardiac orifice.
On the third day, the skin had assumed a lemon
colour, which was first perceptible in the conjunctiva and upper parts of the neck; the heat
had subsided, but the pulse had increased in
frequency; hiccough was urgent. The matters
vomited were mixed with dark flakes, sometimes
resembling snuff, sometimes the dregs of port

wine. Soon after this, two or three pints of a black fluid, like soot and water, were ejected with great force, and death closed the scene. In some cases, the vomiting would cease suddenly, either spontaneously or on the exhibition of an opiate, and violent delirium or coma would supervene.

CASE I.—D. G——, aged twenty-one, engineer, lately arrived from England, October 23, 1835, awoke with a sense of fatigue and pain in his back, which he ascribed to a long walk he had taken the evening before. At noon he was found in a high state of fever, with intense pain over the orbits, red, watery eyes, pulse 100, full and strong. He was bled to thirty ounces, and pills of calomel, compound extract of colocynth, and jalap, were ordered. The bleeding relieved the headache, reduced the pulse to 90, and occasioned a copious diaphoresis. At 4 P.M. headache and febrile heat had returned, and vomiting was urgent. The abstraction of eight ounces of blood was again followed by relief of all the symptoms. The pills were repeated every second hour, with effervescing draughts of the tartrate of soda. 8 P.M.—The fever was less violent; the bowels had not been moved. The hair was cut, and cold affusion applied to the head as often as the heat returned. The medicines were continued.

24th.—Headache and vomiting were still urgent; the medicine had acted but slightly. Five grains of calomel were given every two hours, with solution of sulphate of magnesia in the intervals. A sinapism was applied to the epigastrium. The cold douche was continued.

25th.—The medicines had acted slightly, and heat had abated. There was frequent emission of gas; a yellow tinge of the skin; scanty urine. A blister was applied to the epigastrium; the calomel was continued, and two grains of camphor every two hours.

26th.—He was much easier; had had dark, tar-like stools.

27th.—He was reported to have passed a quiet night, but I found him at 6 A.M. sinking; the skin cold, and pulse scarcely perceptible. Wine and other stimulants were prescribed, but he died at 10 A.M., immediately after ejecting a wash-hand basinful of the black vomit.

Post-mortem Examination at 3 P.M.—The external surface was of a yellow colour, spotted with purple patches.

Abdomen.—The viscera appeared healthy externally. Liver of a natural size; yellow colour. The gall-bladder contained a small quantity of dark-green viscid bile. The stomach contained a pint of black fluid; internal surface highly congested, from cardiac orifice to one and a half inch from pylorus. Small intestines full of black inky fluid, which was warm, and in a state of fermentation. Peyer's glands were very conspicuous; colon stained of a dark livid colour, interspersed with red patches; kidneys healthy. There was half a pint of urine in the bladder.

CASE II.—Mr. S. A——, aged twenty-five. I was called at 11 P.M. on the 8th October, 1842, to visit this young man, a native of Scotland, who had been but a short time in the island. I was informed that he had been complaining of great lassitude all day, with pain in the back and limbs. I found him labouring under intense rachialgia, and incessant jactitation, with much headache and coldness of the lower extremities.

His feet were immersed in hot water, and in that position he was bled to the extent of thirty ounces, with great relief of all the symptoms. His pulse, which before the bleeding was 120, and very small, became fuller and less frequent. His skin became moist, and the temperature more equable. He was ordered to take large doses of calomel, colocynth, and jalap, every two hours till his bowels were emptied. On the morning of the 9th, Dr. Musgrave found him complaining of a return of headache, with an increase of heat, and he thought it advisable to abstract about eight ounces more blood from him. The purgative pills were continued, with the addition of a mixture of the compound powder of jalap, but his bowels were slow in responding. In the course of Monday, the 10th, his stomach became very irritable, and he brought up much larger quantities of fluid than appeared to be ingested. The prescription was a blister to the stomach, five grains of calomel every two hours, with effervescing draughts. On the morning of the 11th he was found much cooler, and quinine was tried, but the irritability of the stomach prevented a continuance of it. Black vomit and hiccough succeeded, and he died at six o'clock in the evening.

CASE III.—Mr. F. P——, aged twenty-one, an Englishman, about two years in the island, was attacked 1st November, 1842, with giddiness and pain in the head and back. When visited the febrile excitement was fully developed. He was bled in the erect position till approaching syncope, when profuse perspiration broke out; the heat was subdued, and all the symptoms relieved. The bowels were freely opened with calomel, colocynth, and jalap. He took ten grains of nitre, with a few drops of spirit. æth. nitros. in a glass of water every two hours. On the 3rd he was in a state of complete apyrexia. Two grains of sulphate of quinine were given every second hour during the day, and on the 6th he was struck off my list as perfectly cured.

CASE IV.—Mrs. P——, wife of the preceding, aged twenty, a native of the island, but who had been some years in England for education, was attacked November 7th, with all the symptoms of the prevailing epidemic, being five months advanced in pregnancy. She was bled to the extent of twenty-four ounces, and treated in every respect like her husband, and on the 12th she was convalescent.

CASE V.—Mr. W. B——, Englishman, aged twenty-five, about three months in the island, was attacked 7th November, 1842, with the usual symptoms of the ardent form of yellow fever then prevailing. He was bled to the extent of forty ounces; was purged with calomel, colocynth, and jalap, and afterwards took effervescing draughts of tartrate of soda, with nitre. On the 10th he was convalescent. He took quinine for three days, after which I took my leave.

II. The ADYNAMIC form was usually met with in females, and persons of a lax fibre and deficient animal vigour. It was ushered in by slight rigors, giddiness, and pain in the back; frequent sighing, and sense of oppression at the præcordia. The reaction which followed was slight, unattended with pungent heat of the skin, or strong arterial action; the pulse was small and compressible. This stage did not last more than forty-eight hours, and was followed by the stage of collapse, great prostration of strength, cold, clammy sweats, feeble pulse, hiccough, vomiting of a dark grumous fluid, yellow colour of the conjunctiva, and a lurid hue of the face. Hæmorrhage from the nose, mouth, anus, and vagina followed, under which the patient sunk in a fit of syncope or asthenia. In others the sensorium was early affected; there was a total suppression of all the secretions: the patient lay tossing about in a state of wild delirium, totally disregarding exposure of her person. Hæmorrhage took place from all the passages; the sheets were stained with blood; her hands were bloody, and her eyes yellow; the arms, legs, and back spotted with vibices. The fairest of creation became an object of pity and abhorrence: in such cases death was hailed with joy by all her attendants.

CASE VI.—Mrs. W——, aged thirty-one, native of Scotland, about three years in the island, was attacked at 5 A.M. on the 10th

October, 1842, with shivering and great pain in
the back, which were soon followed by symptoms of fever of a mild character ; the pulse was
quick and feeble, and the skin warm, but rather
moist. The fever continued during that and
the following day without any urgent symptom,
except a distressing pain in the back. On the
12th she was found free from fever, and a solution of sulphate of quinine was prescribed.
But at 3 P.M. she was suddenly seized with
vomiting, and brought up a pint of *black* fluid ;
after which her pulse began to fail, and symptoms of collapse occurred. At 5 P.M. she had
an epileptic fit; diffusible stimulants were administered liberally; but she remained for several days in a state of extreme exhaustion. On
the 13th, hiccough was added to the other bad
symptoms. On the 14th, the abdomen was
tympanitic, when twenty drops of oleum terebinth. were given every two hours with good
effect. Next day the bowels became relaxed.
The discharges consisted of bloody serum :
these were restrained by tincture of opium and
carbonate of ammonia, and she gradually recovered.

CASE VII.—Mrs. W——, aged twenty-eight, a native of England, from which she had arrived only a few months. This lady's husband was a physician, holding an official situation in the colony, but was not engaged in practice. His mother-in-law died of fever on the 15th October, 1842, never having been considered by him in danger till fatal coma occurred. This unexpected event occasioned much grief to Mrs. W——, and she was preparing to accept the invitation of a friend to spend some time in the country, when I was sent for, on the 25th October. I found her seated on a chair, dressed in mourning, and the carriage at the door ready for the journey. She complained of giddiness, pains in the back, and a total prostration of strength. Her husband was urging her to proceed, protesting that she was suffering only from grief and want of sleep. Her pulse was quick; and there was increased heat about the head and trunk, although her skin was generally moist. I sent her to bed, and called a consultation of her medical friends in two hours, when I hoped reaction would have taken place; and as she was of a plethoric habit, though phlegmatic temperament, the propriety of bloodletting might be a question of intricacy. At our visit, fever was more fully developed, but the state of the pulse did not admit of venesection. Purgatives, into which calomel entered largely, were prescribed, to be repeated at short intervals. Next day there was no distinct change. The following day the febrile symptoms were increased, with much cerebral excitement and constant jactitation. The head was shaven, and the calomel, with camphor, given every two hours. But the symptoms became gradually worse. The delirium was violent, and she was with difficulty retained in the bed. The secretion of urine was suppressed; hæmorrhage took place from the nose, mouth, and vagina; the skin was yellow, and the arms, legs, and depending parts were marked with livid spots. She died on the fifth day. Her husband was attacked with the disease under the *congestive* form on the 27th, and died on the seventh day.

III. The CONGESTIVE form is characterized by the total absence of febrile heat. The patient has a stupid, drunken appearance, will scarcely admit that he is ill, or complains only of slight pain in the back and limbs. He staggers in his gait, or lies in a soporose state. Deafness ensues, and afterwards low muttering delirium. The pulse is at first slow and intermitting; it becomes quicker in the progress of the disease, but seldom exceeds 100. The stools are unnatural, without any admixture of bile; the urine is scanty, and is ultimately suppressed. The skin is of a yellow mottled hue. Hiccough occurs early, with black vomiting, and hæmorrhage from the mouth and nose, and the case usually terminates by convulsions or coma.

CASE VIII.—Mr. F——, a native of the United States, aged thirty-eight, about a week after his arrival in Antigua, in November, 1835, was attacked with slight headache and pain in the limbs, which he said he would scarcely have noticed but for the prevalence of yellow fever in St. John's. His pulse was slow and intermitting. His medical attendant treated him with active doses of calomel; but the bowels were scarcely moved, and the discharges were

destitute of bile. On the third day he became
tinged with a yellow suffusion. On the fourth
I saw him; his pulse was then 96; he had
hiccough, hæmorrhage from the gums, and vomiting of a brownish fluid with dark-coloured
flocculi. The urinary secretion was suppressed.
Being a stranger and a man of family, the mer-
chant to whom he was consigned requested that
we would make known to him our opinion, if we
thought him in danger. This was done in as
considerate terms as possible by his medical
attendant, when he replied very angrily that he
begged leave to differ from us—he was not ill,
and we had quite mistaken his complaint. Next
morning he was found incoherent, sitting up in
bed, and with a fixed melancholy gaze and cor-
rugated brow: blood was issuing from the pores
of the right cheek. He took no notice of us as
we entered his room, but continued repeating
the letters of the alphabet slowly. He died in
the evening, after several convulsions.

Dissection.—On opening the abdomen the
stomach was observed much distended, and pre-
senting on its external aspect several dark spots
like incipient gangrene; but on laying it open,

this was found to be occasioned by the abrasion of the mucous coat in several places, and the presence of a black, inky fluid, like soot and water. The mucous membrane of the upper half of the duodenum was also abraded. The rest of the intestines were sound. The liver was pale; the gall bladder was distended with dark green bile. The lining membrane of the heart was highly injected, and studded with patches of extravasated blood in several places. The sigmoid valves exhibited the same appearance.

ANATOMICAL CHARACTERS.

The yellow colour of the surface of the body was always more distinctly visible after death, and on the depending parts it was mixed with purple patches. All the appearances indicated a defective crasis of the blood : it remained fluid after death. The capillaries of the serous membrane were in a state of hyperæmia, but there was seldom any exudation of *liquor sanguinis* perceptible. The mucous membrane of the upper half of the alimentary canal was generally softened, and the epithelium detached from the stomach and duodenum. The muciparous glands were found enlarged only in one case. The stomach contained always more or less blood, which was changed into a black colour, and frequently mixed with gas. The liver was usually of a pale, bloodless colour, and the spleen presented no unusual appearance. The gall bladder was sometimes turgid with black bile, in other cases it was nearly empty. The thoracic viscera exhibited only such appearances of congestion as were referrible to the fluid state of the blood, and the mode of death. In one case the blood in the right ventricle had a frothy appearance, having been evidently mixed with gas during life.

DIAGNOSIS.

The only diseases with which yellow fever can be confounded are bilious remittent, and the malignant forms of intermittent fever; and as many medical men, for whose opinion I entertain the highest respect, consider all these fevers as the offspring of the same terrestrial miasmata, modified only by the constitution of the individual, and other unknown agents, it is necessary that I should relate more fully the circumstances which have induced me to form a different opinion. My experience is derived entirely from a residence of twenty-five years in Antigua, where intermittent and remittent fevers are en demic, and met with every year, chiefly from September to March, and where yellow fever has only occurred three times during that period. The endemic fevers prevail chiefly in the country districts, and the inhabitants of St. John's are seldom attacked with them. Whereas, the epidemic yellow fever was confined to the city and to the garrison at the Ridge, and at English Harbour. It is difficult to account for the comparative exemption from remittent fever which is enjoyed by the European youths who are employed in the mercantile profession in town, whilst those who superintend agricultural operations in the country, never escape.

Antigua is of a rough circular figure, being 20 miles long and 54 in circumference, containing 108 square miles, equivalent to 69,277 acres; two-thirds of which are under cultivation. There are few springs in the island, and no streams that deserve the name of rivers: but it is much indented with creeks and bays, whose oozy waters maintain the growth of impenetrable thickets of the different species of mangrove, and are the fertile sources of malaria.

In a geological point of view, the island comprises three distinct formations of the tertiary class, of which the most superficial beds occupy the northern and eastern divisions. These consist of a calcareous marl, and coarse sandstone, interspersed with masses of a tolerably compact shell limestone. On the surface are found a great variety of marine exuviæ, analogous to those which at present inhabit the surrounding seas, as astrea, meandrinæ, tubipora, &c. The surface of this district is exceedingly broken and undulated, consisting of a series of round-backed hills of no great elevation, covered with a light arid soil. The sides of the hills and intervening valleys are highly cultivated, and produce a rapid growth when duly favoured with rain.

The mountainous district, forming the southern and western divisions, is composed of rocks of the newest flöetz trap formations, as wacke, porphyry, trap breccia, ampygdaloid, and some spherical masses of basaltic green-stone. Some of these mountains rise with conical summits to the height of 800 to 1000 feet; others, of the same elevation, are more rounded and less precipitous, affording a good soil for the sugar-cane even on the tops. They are intersected by beautifully romantic valleys; and the abrupt sides of the mountains are clothed with the verdant foliage of a great variety of herbs, and trees, and twining shrubs.

The intermediate district is occupied by a series of argillaceous strata of varied characters, which dip at a considerable angle to the north and north-east, and extend across the island from Willoughby Bay on the south-east, to St. John's in the north-west. The northern limit of this district is formed by a zone of low land, which at no very distant period, appears to have been submerged, and even now, after heavy rains, is readily converted into a marsh. It rises with a gentle acclivity towards the south and south-west, where it presents a precipitous escarpment, and is divided from the trap formation by a ravine, in which are pools of stagnant water, and a sluggish stream which runs towards the west, through a beautifully luxuriant plain.

Although this district, and the mangrove creeks with which the island is indented, present the only unequivocal sources of paludal emanations, yet all parts of the island are at certain seasons affected by malaria—the dry, calcareous soil of the north, equally with the humid valleys of the south. How is this to be explained? Two things are always present when fever prevails in these districts—a hot sun during the day, and circumstances favourable to the radiation of heat from the earth, and the deposition of dew at night.

The febrific poison, whatever it may be, appears to be deposited with the dew, even at a distance from its source ; and all who are subjected to its influence, as it rises again at the approach of the sun, are as much affected as if they had inhaled it at the fountain-head. This is the only way in which I can explain the greater prevalence of fever in country districts than in St. John's; it being well known that more dew is deposited in the open country than in cities, where houses conceal a portion of the sky. A soil covered with vegetation is also more favourable to the production of dew, than the trodden streets of a town. At these seasons, the mean dew point is about 70°; bu&, in the cloudless moonlight nights, the thermometer falls sometimes to 66°, producing an unpleasant sensation of cold, of which the inhabitants of northern latitudes, who enjoy a temperature some degrees lower than this, can scarcely form an idea.* The injurious effects of dew have been long

* Dr. Chisholm, in his "Manual of Tropical Dis-eases," mentions this peculiarity of temperature in Antigua; but, in my opinion, he has overlooked the true cause. He says: "Antigua, being altogether argillaceous, is distinguished by a peculiarity in the temperature of its atmosphere; it is a degree of cold not observed in any of the other islands, but which has, on the human body, all the influence of marsh exhalation, although no swamps are in the neighbour-hood of St. John's, where this singular cold is chiefly felt, after rain has continued to fall for a few hours. On these occasions Fahrenheit's thermometer falls to 62°." (p. 2.)—Now, I have never observed the ther-mometer below 64°, and it was always in the driest seasons and in cloudless moonlight nights, and gene-rally in the month of February, *not after rain*, when this unusually low temperature occurred. Antigua is one of the driest of the West Indian islands, and to this circumstance and the low dew-point I attribute the descent of the thermometer where terrestrial radia-tion is great. Professor Fleming, on the "Temperature

known to the vulgar ; and I think it has been unjustly overlooked by the late Dr. William Fergusson, in his interesting paper on "Marsh Poison."

The city is built on the north-west part of the island, occupying an area of 161 acres, and contains a population of about 9000 souls. The principal streets are wide, and run from east to west, having a gentle declivity towards the sea or harbour. The highest part of the town being about 40 feet above the tide level. They are crossed at right angles by other streets not quite so wide. They are macadamized with broken stones, composed chiefly of indurated marl, and the gutters on each side are mostly paved. Nevertheless, in consequence of the impermeable

of the Seasons," observes : " Where the air is very dry, or where the dew-point is very low, the descent of the evening branch of the curve will be prolonged, in the absence of the counteracting curve which has been referred to—viz., the caloric given out when vapour is converted into dew—and in consequence the cold of the night may be great. But when the air is humid, or, in ordinary language, nearly saturated with moisture, and the dew-point consequently high, then the sinking of the evening temperature is prevented from exceeding in any considerable degree that point at which the existing vapour must be converted into water." (p. 22.)

nature of the sub-soil, the streets in the lower part of the city are very swampy after heavy rains. Attempts have been made to correct this by sinking deep wells in various parts, which furnish a supply of water useful for many purposes, but it is too much impregnated with saline matter for internal use. All the public buildings and the larger houses have tanks or cisterns attached to them, in which the rain-water collected from the roofs is preserved; and at the south-east corner of the city there is a large pond, from which the poorer inhabitants are supplied.

The principal cemetery of the parish occupies the highest part of the city, and there are two other burying-places within its boundaries, one at the north, the other at the south.

The land immediately to the east of the city, to the extent of half a mile, is not under cultivation, but on the south and north the cane fields approach its immediate precincts.

So much for the extrinsic cause of endemic fevers. Let us next inquire whether these fevers may be so far modified by constitutional peculiarities in the European, as to assume the *con-*

tinued or *malignant* form of yellow fever. Since the year 1837, a considerable number of English labourers have been imported into Antigua, which has afforded me an opportunity of seeing this question put to the test of experiment; and, although they have suffered more or less from *fièvre du pays,* not one case of black vomit has come to my knowledge. In May, 1843, twenty-six English tradesmen were imported by a wealthy mercantile firm, for the purpose of re-building those works which were destroyed by the earthquake on the 8th of February of that year.   They were lodged in the country, in a house sufficiently roomy, and in every respect commodious, but in a locality much exposed to *malaria.*   Their employer, considering the heat of the sun the only thing likely to be prejudicial to the health of these unacclimated strangers, allowed them to retire to their house for three hours at noon; but they entered on their work before sunrise in the morning. They were all attacked in a short time with remittent fever, of the most aggravated type, attended with a deep yellow colour of the surface, delirium, &c.; yet they all recovered without hæmorrhage from the mucous passages, black vomit, or any symptoms indicative of that dyscrasia of the blood peculiar to yellow fever.*

Again, in 1845 about thirty mechanics were imported to rebuild our cathedral, which was destroyed by the same visitation. They were located in St. John's, where they remained upwards of two years; and not one of them was attacked with fever—another proof of the greater prevalence of the endemic in the country than in town, and also that an unseasoned constitution is not sufficient to convert remittent into the continued yellow fever.

I am desirous of confining my remarks to what came under my own observation, otherwise I might add, that yellow fever occurs where marsh fevers are not known, as on board of ships at sea, in the garrison at Barbadoes, at Vera Cruz, &c.

Are there no symptoms by which yellow fever

---

* One old man died afterwards in the Colonial Infirmary, of the sequelæ of the fever; and I have heard that some of the others died of dropsical symptoms on the passage to England, no doubt from organic diseases of the abdominal viscera produced by the fever.

may be distinguished from other forms of tropical
fever?   At the commencement of this disease,
there are no symptoms by which it can be distinguished from an attack of the endemic, or even
any other ephemeral fever arising from atmospheric changes.   The suffusion of the eyes,
pain in the head and back, closely resemble the
precursory symptoms of influenza.   It is only
in the progress of the disease, when the torpid
state of the secretory glands, the chlorotic hue of
the skin, and hæmorrhage from the mucous surfaces, reveal the nature of the epidemic. Whether
the morbid state of the blood, which forms the
pathognostic symptom of this fever, is the immediate effect of its contamination with a poisonous
principle from *without*, or merely the consequence of defective elimination of effete matter
generated *within* the body, is a question that
has not yet been determined.   Probably this
change in the vital fluid is attributable to both
causes.

It is very evident that the first link in the
concatenation of morbid phenomena is congestion of the capillaries of the brain, spinal cord,
and abdominal viscera; and the great benefit

derived from blood-letting at the commencement of the attack, so as to remove this state of congestion, would seem to prove that it is the chief proximate cause of the disease. On the other hand, the great susceptibility of Europeans, who have never had the disease, and the immunity of those who have once had it, and of those whose blood has been modified by a long residence in a warm climate, look like the operations of a morbid poison on certain substances, which may exist in the blood of one individual, and not in another.

The yellow colour which attends bilious remittent is generally, if not always, produced by excessive secretion of bile, and the reabsorption of some of it into the blood : notwithstanding, a large quantity is duly excreted, as shown by the colour of the stools, which varies from a deep yellow to a dark green. Some doubts have been entertained recently whether excretions from the bowels of a green colour are due to bile ; but of this no practitioner in the West Indies can possibly have any doubt.

Louis, in his observations on the yellow fever of Gibraltar, has laid much stress on a peculiar

colour of the liver as a diagnostic character.
Nothing very remarkable to the naked eye was
observed in Antigua fever, except in some cases
its anæmic colour, and we had no means at this
time of making a microscopic examination.

Not the least remarkable feature in the history
of yellow fever, is the fact, generally admitted,
that it attacks an individual only once in his
lifetime.   This was in great measure corrobo-
rated by the epidemics that fell under my notice ;
not one of those persons who suffered in the first
epidemic was attacked in the subsequent visita-
tions.

TREATMENT.

When the epidemic began in 1835, it was
treated on the general principle pursued in the
treatment of fevers within the tropics.   At the
first visit, if the symptoms were sufficiently
urgent, and particularly if the patient was a
European, in whom the tone of the vascular
system was unimpaired, blood was drawn in suf·
ficient quantity to produce a decided impression
on the system, as indicated by relief of the headache and pain in the back, reduction of the pulse,

and a general diaphoresis; an active purgative of calomel, compound extract of colocynth, and jalap, was administered, and repeated every two or three hours till a satisfactory discharge from the bowels was produced; the action of the kidneys was stimulated by small doses of nitre, frequently repeated, and the head and chest were assiduously sponged with cold water. When these measures failed to relieve the febrile symptoms, and to rouse the liver to increased secretion, five grains of calomel were given every two hours. Vomiting was arrested by the application of rubefacient of capsicum or mustard, or sometimes of a blister to the epigastrium, aided with saline effervescents, or a draught of magnesia, tincture of opium, and mint water.

The following case, however, created a strong prejudice against blood-letting, and the mercurial treatment was chiefly confided in after that. Calomel was given in some cases to the extent of 250 grains, without any sensible effect on the system; and it could generally be detected at the bottom of the vessel containing the watery stools, in the form of black oxide. . .

CASE IX.—Mrs. B——, a native of England, aged thirty-five, was attacked on October 4th, 1835, with symptoms of the prevailing fever. Her husband, in his youth, had been some time in an apothecary's shop, and still retained a love for the profession, which he displayed occasionally by the practice of minor surgical operations, such as bleeding and extraction of teeth, for the benefit of his friends. On the evening of the 4th he made various ineffectual attempts to draw blood from Mrs. B——, and on the 5th I was sent for. I found her labouring under symptoms of a mild attack of the fever, and venesection might have been considered unnecessary; but to please her husband, and at the same time, perhaps, not a little influenced by a desire of convincing him that he was not an expert surgeon, I abstracted about sixteen ounces of blood at a full stream. This depletion appeared to be well borne, and the headache and other febrile symptoms were much relieved. She had already taken purgative medicine, and a mild febrifuge was all that was considered necessary. Her husband was attacked the following day, and I myself on the 7th, having left Mrs. B—— apparently convalescent.

On the morning of the 9th she was so well that she got up, and went into the adjoining bed-room where Mr. B—— was lying. She sat for some time on his bed, endeavouring to comfort him with religious conversation, and expressing her gratitude that she had so far recovered as to be able to attend to him. On returning to her chamber, she discovered that she had a discharge which she took for the catamenia. Soon afterwards she was attacked with syncope. Messengers were sent in every direction for medical men, and three were very soon at her bedside, but the vital spark had fled. Two of these medical men were strongly opposed to the use of the lancet in fever, and it was very currently reported that Mrs. B—— had fallen a victim to this rash practice; and the effect on the public mind was such that to propose such a measure afterwards was met with horror both by the patient and his friends.

The lancet was not used in any of the cases that died subsequently, except that of D. G——, already described (page 11).

In the epidemic of 1839, when the *ardent* form prevailed, and also in 1842, blood-letting was had recourse to at the commencement of the attack, with great benefit, and, in some cases, *to* a very large extent.

Our assistant, Dr. C——, lost about sixty ounces of blood, and my son not much less, and, in a few days, they were both convalescent. However, it is only within the first twelve hours from the commencement of the hot stage that this bold treatment is admissible. If the congestion in the capillary system is not removed by the early and decided use of the lancet, the blood soon becomes so disorganized, and the tone of the extreme vessels so destroyed, that the loss of even a few ounces cannot be borne with safety.

CASE X.—Mr. C——, aged twenty-three, a native of England, had been about six weeks in the island when he was attacked with symptoms of yellow fever, on the 8th October, 1842. He had been confined to his bed, and under treatment for a sprained ankle, for some days previously, so that the first twelve hours of the fever were overlooked. On the morning of the 9th he was bled, but a tendency to syncope occurred before eight ounces of blood had flowed. His pulse was never above 90. On the 10th he had black vomit, and the stage of collapse commenced. His skin was yellow and mottled with livid spots. Wine and porter were given liberally, and for a time he appeared to be recovering his strength; but on the evening of the 11th the wound in his arm burst out bleeding, which was not observed till his pulse was nearly extinguished. He died at midnight.

In the *asthenic* form blood-letting was of course never thought of; and in the *congestive*, I never had the courage to make the trial. In the latter moments, diffusible stimulants, rubefacients, and blisters were the remedies used, but they were generally as ineffectual as if they had been applied to a dead body.

During convalescence quinine was always administered, to the extent of six or eight grains of the disulphate daily, and the dietetic regimen required the utmost attention.

APPENDIX.

THE foregoing Essay was written in the early part of 1849, and presented to the Faculty of Medicine in the University of Glasgow as a graduation thesis. On my return to Antigua in November of that year, I found that yellow fever was prevailing amongst the European troops to a most fatal extent, the surgeon and many of the men of the 54th Regiment having fallen victims. On this occasion it was remarkable that the civilians unconnected with the garrison were entirely exempt from the epidemic. Indeed, the poisonous atmosphere appeared to be confined within very small limits, being confined to the Ridge, the chief military station, situated on the south-east part of the island, on a hill of 800 or 900 feet elevation, bounded by the sea on the east and south, and overlooking English

Harbour and the Dockyard on the west. The northern boundary is occupied by an extensive tract of uncultivated land, covered with thickets of brushwood. After a time the troops were removed, and placed under tents at Monk's Hill, an old military post about four miles to the westward of the Ridge, and about the same elevation. It presents an abrupt precipice to the south, which shows it to be composed chiefly of trap breccia and conglomerate, capped by a stratified rock of a beautiful sea-green colour, containing crystals of augite and other minerals.* Here the disease gradually abated; but it was some weeks before the poison imbibed at the Ridge was entirely eliminated from the system, as cases occurred among the men daily for some time after their removal. One officer, who was on a visit to a gentleman in the neighbourhood of St. John's, fell under our care. He was bled by my son at the very onset of the attack, and treated with active mercurial purgatives and

---

* This rock was mistaken by Dr. Chisholm many years ago for an ore of copper, and formed the basis of his theory of fish-poison.—*Edin. Med. and Surg. Journ.*, vol. iv. p. 393.

saline refrigerants and diuretics. On the third day he was convalescent, and taking quinine; the only symptom of disease remaining being a remarkably slow pulse. Another officer, a young Irishman of gigantic stature and robust frame, was seized whilst on duty at Monk's Hill. Having witnessed the speedy recovery of his comrade, he was most anxious to come to town to be placed under our care. At length the colonel yielded to his wishes, and he was conveyed in a four-wheeled carriage, accompanied by an assistant-surgeon.

When I saw him it was too late for general bleeding; but his intense headache, ferret-like eyes, and bounding pulse, induced me to have him cupped on the nape of the neck. This produced apparent relief; but the case was attended from the first with an obstinate diarrhœa, which resisted the use of calomel and opium, acetate of lead, and similar remedies. Nevertheless, he survived the critical days on which death usually occurs, and we began to entertain hopes that he might struggle through it, when suddenly he was attacked with delirium, the stools assumed the colour and appearance of black vomit, and he died on the ninth day.

A melancholy case occurred in the family of an engineer officer, who was about to return to England in the next steamer. He fled to St. John's with his wife and daughter, a young lady in the full bloom of health and beauty. A day or two after her arrival in the city, this young lady was attacked with the disease, and died on the fifth day.

Five artillerymen were removed to the barrack in St. John's on the 30th November. Next day two of them sickened, and the following day the three others. They were under the care of my friend Dr. Furlonge, who has published an account of them in the *Lancet* for 1850. One died on the fifth, and another on the seventh day; the rest recovered.

I have heard much during the last three years of the successful treatment of yellow fever in Demerara by large doses of quinine and calomel; twenty-four grains of the former and twenty grains of the latter being the usual dose. This practice is so contrary to what I consider the rational treatment of ardent fevers, that I could not in my conscience adopt it in such cases. I might venture to try it in the congestive form of the disease; and, perhaps, that is the type most prevalent in the swampy colonies of Guiana.

Dr. Blair has had ample opportunities recently of testing the efficacy of this empirical treatment; and the profession may justly claim from him a report of his extended experience. It is to be hoped, also, that he will publish the result of another experiment he has been making, with the view of protecting individuals from the disease by administering belladonna as a prophylactic.*

* These remarks, with regard to the *abortive* treatment with quinine, were written in January, 1853; since then Dr. Blair has fully responded to the call, and has published, in the January and April numbers of the "British and Foreign Medico-Chirurgical Review," an elaborate report on the last epidemic in Guiana, in which he has availed himself of the most recent improvements in chemical and physical science in investigating and describing the phenomena of the disease, and has arrived at the following hypothetical conclusion: "The efficient cause of the disease known as yellow fever is an aërial poison, probably organic, which requires a certain temperature for its generation and existence, and affects special localities and persons. This poison attaches itself to the mucous surfaces of

Yellow fever broke out in Antigua on the
15th of May, 1853,* in the person of a delicate
female, a native of Scotland, who had been only
eighteen months or two years in the island.
This case was reported to me by an express
from my son, when I was at St. Kitt's, whither
I had gone for change of air, having suffered
for some months from a severe attack of acute
rheumatism. No other case occurred for several
days; but when I arrived, on June 3rd, I learnt
that my son had two other cases on his list—
one, a young Scotchman, who resided not many

the human body. One of the primary effects of such
contact, when the quantity is adequate, is to rouse the
system into febrile reaction, and to excite through the
stomach and intestines an effort to expel the noxious
agent. There is reason to believe that this expulsory
effort is sometimes successful unassisted, but is mate-
rially aided by the action of certain medicinal substances. In the event of the expulsory effort being
unsuccessful, the effect of this poison is to act destruc-
tively on the epithelial structures of the body by in-
ducing a specific irritation in the basement membrane,
by which, and by allied consecutive lesions, the arterial
and capillary tissues are impaired, the viscera become
congested, the blood thereby contaminated by suppressed secretions, and fatal hæmorrhages ensue."

* May is usually the healthiest month in the year.

yards from the house in which the first case occurred; the other, an army surgeon, living in another part of the city.

I saw both patients on the morning of the 5th. I found Dr. D—— labouring under intense headache; his features were red and turgid, the vessels of the conjunctiva much injected, and his pulse 112, full and bounding. I learnt that he had not been bled, for what appeared satisfactory reasons; but, on the contrary, he had taken 29 grains of quinine with calomel the day before, his bowels having been previously acted upon by pills of calomel, colocynth, and croton oil. A blister was applied to the neck, calomel administered every two hours, alternately with effervescing saline draughts. On the 6th the heat had subsided and the headache was relieved, but the evacuations were discovered to be destitute of bile; quinine and calomel were prescribed, but he became gradually worse, and died on the 8th with black vomit.

The young Scotchman was treated in the same way; he was not bled, and he had suppression of urine, black vomit, and died on the 7th, the fifth day of the disease.

E

The next fatal case that came under my observation, was that of a young gentleman who arrived from Liverpool on the 5th to take charge of a mercantile concern in the city. He sickened on the 9th, when an unsuccessful attempt to bleed him was made by his medical attendant. When I saw him, on the 11th, the second stage had commenced. On the 13th, he had petechiæ and black vomit, and died on the 14th. Two of the crew belonging to the ship in which this gentleman arrived were brought to the hospital on the 13th, labouring under fever. The first was bled very unsatisfactorily, and he died on the fifth day; the other was bled *ad deliquium*, and recovered.

The first severe case which I saw from the beginning, was that of a young Scotchman employed in a mercantile establishment, who was attacked on the 15th June. He was bled from the arm to the extent of thirty ounces, when vomiting occurred with profuse perspiration, and complete relief of all the symptoms. Within an hour the headache and pain in the back returned, and the pulse became more frequent than before the bleeding. He was then treated with calomel, saline effervescing draughts, the application of sinapisms and blisters, the cold douche, &c. There was complete suppression of the biliary and urinary secretions, and he died with black vomit on the 19th.

CASE XI.—W.B——, Esq., aged twenty-five, had been occupied in St. John's all day on the 23rd of June, and rode home in the evening to his residence in the country, a distance of five miles. Soon after midnight, he was attacked with the usual symptoms of the epidemic. My son visited him about 4 A.M., and bled him largely. The bleeding was followed by immediate relief of the headache, and such a profuse perspiration that it was several hours before his father could venture to remove him to St. John's, which he was most anxious to do. When he arrived, between eleven and twelve o'clock, he had a return of headache, and although the pungent heat of skin had not returned, the pulse was 120, and small.

Finding after two or three hours' rest, and the free action of the bowels, that the symptoms had not improved, I set this case down as a bad one, and proposed a consultation with another medical friend. When we visited him, on the morning of the 25th, the headache was then the most urgent symptom. A blister was applied to the forehead, and calomel, in five-grain doses, given every second hour, with saline draughts in the intervals. The bowels acted freely, discharging large quantities of a dark green fluid, like the expressed juice of plants. There was a copious flow of urine also.

On the 26th, the fever had subsided, and the headache was so much relieved that quinine was tried. A single dose increased the headache so much, that it was stopped, and a blister applied to the neck. The calomel was resumed till he had taken 120 grains. On the 27th, a dose of castor-oil was given with good effect. On the 28th he was so much better, that we were induced to give a favourable prognosis to his anxious parent when he was closing his letter for the European mail. Soon afterwards, however, he began to complain of acute pain in the umbilical region, nevertheless, his pulse was only 80. A large blister was applied, and a draught, containing rhubarb and magnesia, with tincture of hyoscyamus, was administered. On inquiry, we found that he had made no water since morning, and there was none in the bladder. 29th.—Two stools, of the consistence and colour of oat-meal gruel, were passed, but no urine. The calomel was resumed, in smaller doses, and the abdomen covered with ung. hydrargyri, acetate of potash with spirit. æther. nitrosi was prescribed till the hour of consultation, when a dose of castor-oil, with ol. terebinth. was given, and the latter repeated every two hours. Hæmorrhage from the nose and mouth occurred, and afterwards black vomit. About 1 A.M. on the 30th he had a severe convulsion, and a second at 5 A.M., after which he remained in a comatose state till he died at 8 A.M.

CASE XII.—On the morning of Sunday, the 26th June, his Excellency the Governor was attacked. When I saw him, at 10 A.M., his head was exceedingly hot, and the branches of the temporal artery throbbing violently. He was quite confused in his intellect, not knowing the day of the week, nor the hour of the day. He was bled in the erect position to the extent of thirty ounces, when he vomited and perspired largely. The headache and febrile heat were removed, and never returned to any great extent. He passed the same green stuff as W. B——, and recovered gradually.

CASE XIII.—B. L——, the private secretary, was attacked on the 28th. He was bled also, and treated in every respect like the two previous cases, but he passed no bile, and there was suppression of urine from the commencement. The irritability of stomach continued in spite of every remedy, blisters, creasote mixture, champagne, ether, acetate of lead with opium, and he died on the 2nd July, having had black vomit and melæna some hours before death.

This epidemic was confined to the city of St. John's. I am not aware of a single case of genuine yellow fever having occurred in an individual that had not been within the atmosphere of the city, except one, and this would be seized upon by the advocates of contagion in support of their doctrine.

One young Scotchman, when convalescent from an attack of the fever, was removed for change of air to Parham, a village six miles distant. The following day, a young man lodging in the same house, who had not been in St. John's for three months, was attacked with the fever, and died with black vomit on the fifth day.

The cause of the eruption of the epidemic is a great mystery. There were no meteorological phenomena to account for it, except that the weather was very hot for the season of the year, and the wind more southerly than usual. There had been a great fall of rain in the end of April and the beginning of May, but when I arrived the weather was dry. The thermometer ranged daily from 84° to 88°, and the dew-point seldom exceeded 78°. The barometer was remarkably high, the column of mercury standing usually one-tenth above 30 inches.

The following table contains an abstract of all the cases which I attended myself, or with my son, exclusive of those I saw in consultation with other medical men :—

Race.	Recovered.	Died.	Total.
Europeans (Adults) . . .	23	... 9	... 32
White Creoles (Adults) .	3	... 0	... 3
„ (Children) .	6	... 2	... 8
Mixed race (Adults) . .	0	... 0	... 0
„ (Children . .	5	... 1	... 6
American	1	... 0	... 1
Portuguese	2	... 1	... 3
	40	13	53

The type of this epidemic, in all cases that came under my observation, was certainly that of the *ardent* form. I did not meet with a single case of the *apyretic* or *congestive* type, such as I have witnessed in former epidemics. The patient was most frequently seized in the morning. No decided rigor was ·observed, but he awoke with a feeling of having slept heavily, as if from a narcotic. This was immediately followed by intense headache and pain in the back; the vessels of the conjunctiva became injected and red; the force and velocity of the pulse great, and the heat of the surface pungent. At this period the tongue presented no unusul appearance. About the third day the febrile heat subsided; the cheeks, which had been of a florid red colour, assumed a darker hue; the lips were red, and the gums spongy and very vascular; the hands and nails became livid, and, when pressed upon, it was long before the blood re-turned to the cutaneous vessels. By-and-by a yellow tinge was perceptible on the conjunctiva, and on each side of the nose, which spread gra-dually over the neck and chest. Hæmorrhage from the nose and mouth now took place; flatu-lency was very distressing; and the vomiting, which was distressing from the first, now be-came more urgent, and, in the fatal cases, the matter ejected was mixed with dark flakes, like the lees of port wine, which gradually became blacker and more copious till death closed the scene. In those cases which terminated favour-ably the discharges from the bowels were copious, and of the darkest sap-green, and the urine was abundant and of a good colour. In fatal cases the motions had not the slightest tinge of green or yellow, and they exhaled an offensive odour like putrid albumen. In those cases the urine was frequently suppressed, and symptoms of *uræmia* were more or less apparent.

None of the cases in my own practice pre-sented unequivocal marks of *petechiæ*, but a military officer, under the care of Dr. Furlonge, was spotted like a leopard from head to foot; even the mucous membrane of the mouth exhibited the same symptoms of extravasation.

Death occurred most frequently on the fifth day; one died on the fourth day, two on the sixth, and one on the seventh day. In those cases in which the urinary secretion was not suspended, death took place by *asthenia*, the patient retaining his intellect till the last. When uræmia existed convulsions and coma preceded death.

From a variety of causes, no *post-mortem* examinations were made.

Treatment.—When I arrived, I found the lancet had not been used in any case; but purgatives, and five-grain doses of quinine, frequently repeated, with the usual auxiliaries, were chiefly confided in. The quinine so administered appeared to me decidedly injurious, and it was abandoned.

In simple cases, where there was no symptom of local congestion or inflammation, purgatives of calomel, colocynth, and jalap, saline refrige-

rants, and effervescing draughts, formed the chief
medicinal treatment. In more severe cases, five
grains of calomel were interposed every two
hours. The cold douche was always most agree-
able to the patient, and was constantly had recourse to in the first stage. When the headache continued beyond the second day, blisters
were applied to the neck or forehead with good
effect.

In all cases, in which at my first visit there
were symptoms of cerebral or hepatic congestion,
or when the force of the circulation was so great
as to threaten destruction to the capillary system, I had recourse to blood-letting; and, if we
may judge of the propriety of the operation by
the rules laid down by Dr. Marshall Hall, we
must decide in its favour, although it did not
always cure the disease. The loss of blood was
well borne in every case. In one patient only
was syncope induced, after the loss of twenty-
four ounces, and he rapidly recovered. In all
the other cases a much larger quantity of blood
was drawn, whilst the patient was in a sitting
posture, and syncope did not occur. The effect
produced was vomiting, copious perspiration,

bleaching of the eyes, and relief of the headache. When permanent reduction of the pulse followed these effects, the case invariably did well; but when the velocity of the pulse continued, the case proved a bad one, and, in my opinion, would have resisted every kind of treatment.

To prove that blood-letting did not do harm, I would mention that it was had recourse to only in the worst cases, and yet not one of these died before the fifth day, whilst two of them lived till the sixth, and one till the seventh day. Of twelve cases in which the lancet was used, six recovered, and six died. In no case was the operation repeated; and it is a question whether the advocates of this practice would not have deemed it right to repeat the operation at a short interval, when the pulse continued quick. But the prejudice which has been excited by modern writers against large detractions of blood in fevers deterred me.

Having lost in succession four cases in which blood-letting was performed, either by myself or in my presence, with all the immediate effects which follow a successful operation, I considered that I was then bound conscientiously to try the

empirical or abortive treatment, with large doses
of quinine and calomel, as recommended by Dr.
Blair of Demerara. The first case that occurred
for this trial was that of a young Scotchman,
who had recently come to the island. The
second dose produced great congestion of the
brain, and a stupor from which he could scarcely
be roused, and he died on the fourth day.
Nevertheless, our next case was treated in the
same way, with twenty grains of calomel and
twenty-four grains of quinine. Great drowsiness
was the immediate result, and we were deterred
from continuing the practice. We resumed our
former mode of treatment, and the patient recovered.

It is unnecessary to enter upon the treatment
that was pursued after hæmorrhages and black
vomit occurred ; I have no confidence then in
any medicinal astringent, or in anything but the
most diligent exhibition of diffusible stimulants.
Patients have sometimes recovered after all
hope was abandoned. This was. the case with
two seamen, who were landed here from a ship
bound from St. Thomas to Barbadoes. They
were in the last stage of the disease, with

hæmorrhages from the nose, mouth, and anus, and black vomit, when admitted into the Infirmary. Sulphate of alum with quinine, tannic acid, and acetate of lead, were successively prescribed; but I discovered that they took nothing freely except their wine.

THE END.